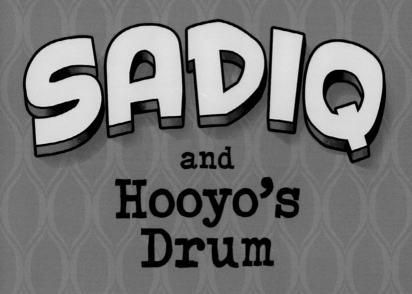

SADIQ

and
Hooyo's
Drum

BY SIMAN NUURALI

ART BY CHRISTOS SKALTSAS

PICTURE WINDOW BOOKS
a capstone imprint

Published by Picture Window Books, an imprint of Capstone.
1710 Roe Crest Drive
North Mankato, Minnesota 56003
capstonepub.com

Library of Congress Cataloging-in-Publication Data is available on
the Library of Congress website.
ISBN: 9781484671153 (hardcover)
ISBN: 9781484674123 (paperback)
ISBN: 9781484674130 (ebook PDF)

Summary: Sadiq is looking forward to being a drummer in the school band
when he's old enough. When Hooyo shows Sadiq a family heirloom—a
drum called a durbaan—Sadiq can't wait to show his mother's drum to
his friends at school. His new friend Gabi, who's deaf, shares his love of
drums. But then a mishap occurs with Hooyo's durbaan. How will Sadiq
explain it to Hooyo, and can he make things right?

Designer: Tracy Davies

Design Elements: Shutterstock/Irtsya

Printed and bound in the USA. 5195

TABLE OF CONTENTS

FACTS ABOUT SOMALIA

- Somali people come from many different clans.
- Many Somalis are nomadic. That means they travel from place to place. They search for water, food, and land for their animals.
- Somalia is mostly desert. It doesn't rain often there.
- The camel is an important animal to Somali people. Camels can survive a long time without food or water.
- Around ninety-nine percent of all Somalis are Muslim.

SOMALI TERMS

ayeeyo (ah-YEH-yoh)—grandmother

baba (BAH-baah)—a common word for father

bariis (buh-REESS)—rice

durbaan (durr-BAHN)—drum

hilib (HIH-lib)—meat

hooyo (HOY-yoh)—mother

qalbi (KUHL-bee)—my heart

vuvuzela (voo-voo-ZELL-ah)—a plastic horn

wiilkeyga (wil-KAY-gaah)—my son

CHAPTER 1

MANY CHOICES

Sadiq heard soft low tones in a pretty melody coming from his sister's room. Then he heard a loud squeak.

"Hi Aliya!" he said, poking his head into his sister's room. She was practicing her clarinet. "Can I come in?"

"Sure! Come on in," replied Aliya. "You can be my audience!" She shuffled through her music.

"I wish I was in band," said Sadiq with a sigh. "It looks like so much fun. Too bad I can't join until fifth grade."

"Fifth grade will be here before you know it!" said Aliya, trying to cheer up her brother.

"I guess you're right," said Sadiq, smiling. "Only two years to go."

"You know what you could do?" asked Aliya. "You could start researching which instrument you'd like to play. That way you'll be ready when the time comes."

"Great idea, Aliya!" said Sadiq. Excitement began to replace his disappointment. "There are so many choices. I wonder what I should pick."

"Well, you have three groups to choose from," said Aliya. "Woodwinds, like my clarinet. Some woodwinds have a wooden reed. You have to have a lot of *wind* to blow into them!"

"Oh cool!" said Sadiq. "I'm good at blowing up balloons. I bet I'd be good at those!"

Aliya laughed. "Next is brass. Trumpets, trombones—all the gold, shiny ones."

"But don't you blow in those too?" asked Sadiq, confused. "They should call those *brass winds!*"

Aliya laughed again. "The last group is percussion—the ones you beat on like a . . ."

"Like a drum?" interrupted Sadiq, his eyes lighting up. His excitement grew even more.

"Exactly," replied Aliya. "Like a drum or a tambourine."

"That would be so fun!" said Sadiq. He jumped up and drummed his hands against Aliya's pillow like he was playing a bongo.

"What's all the noise?" asked Nuurali, coming into the room. "I heard you all the way down the hall."

"Well I *was* practicing . . ." said Aliya, grinning. "Until someone decided to do a drum solo on my pillow."

"I'm going to play drums in band when I get to fifth grade!" Sadiq said.

"That's a *loooooong* way away," said Nuurali. He playfully patted Sadiq's head.

"I could learn to play now," said Sadiq, ducking from his brother. "Then I'll be a drumming machine by fifth grade!"

"I think you should play the *vuvuzela*," teased Nuurali. He pretended to hold up the big plastic horn that played just one tone. "You'd only have to learn one note!"

"Ha ha ha," replied Sadiq. "Very funny."

"My school is hosting a musical festival next weekend," said Nuurali. "There will be all kinds of instruments and music. Want to come?"

"Sure!" replied Sadiq. "Are you looking for an instrument to play too?"

"Not me!" Nuurali said. "I prefer *dancing* to the music. I have all the best moves, as you know."

Nuurali clapped his hands, did the moonwalk across the floor, and ended in a spin.

"Oh, that's nothing," bragged Sadiq. "Look at *my* moves!"

He crab-walked over to the window and then popped back up to standing.

The brothers high-fived each other and laughed.

"Everyone knows I have the best moves of all," said Aliya. "But I am too busy practicing to show you."

"Okay, let's hear it, Aliya," said Nuurali. "Play us your amazing clarinet."

"Prepare to be blown away," said Aliya. "The song is called 'Birds Singing.'"

"More like 'Cats Screeching,' I bet," said Nuurali. Aliya tossed a pillow at him.

"Kids!" *Hooyo* called up from the foot of the stairs. "Dinner is ready. Would you come set the table please?"

"Yes, Hooyo!" the three called out together.

"You'll have to play us your bird song later, Aliya," said Sadiq.

Then Nuurali made a sound like a terrified cat as he bounded down the stairs. Sadiq and Aliya chased after him.

CHAPTER 2

NEW STUDENTS

Sadiq, Manny, and Zaza were walking to school the next morning.

"Have you guys thought about band?" asked Sadiq.

"Like rock bands? Or the school band?" asked Zaza.

"School band," Sadiq said. "I'm planning to join. But I don't want to wait until fifth grade. I want to learn an instrument now."

"You'd be good at that, Sadiq!" said Manny.

"What instrument do you want to play?" asked Zaza.

"I think I want to play drums. But I haven't decided for sure, yet."

"Well now I want to join band too," said Zaza, grinning.

"It would be so fun to do together!" said Sadiq.

"My baby sister bangs on a pot at home. Maybe she can give you drum lessons!" Zaza joked.

***

When the boys got to class, they saw two new students and a woman standing next to Ms. Battersby.

"I wonder who they are?" asked Zaza.

"I am sure we'll find out," said Sadiq.

"Take your seats, children," said Ms. Battersby. "Quickly now. I'd like to introduce you to Gabi and Angie. They're twins and will be joining our class. Let's give them a big welcome!"

"Welcome, Gabi and Angie!" the students called out, waving and clapping.

"Hi, I'm Angie!" said the shorter twin.

Then Gabi began moving her hands. The woman next to them spoke while Gabi signed with her hands.

"Hi everyone! I'm Gabi. I am deaf and use American Sign Language to communicate."

"I know ASL too," Angie said while she signed with her hands. "That's short for American Sign Language."

"I can read lips most of the time," Gabi signed while the woman spoke. "I have an interpreter who helps me. Her name is Ms. Sarah."

Then Ms. Sarah waved and added, "Hello children. I am so happy to meet you all. I am here to help interpret when needed."

"Hello, Ms. Sarah!" said the students, excited to have *three* new people in their class.

"Please tell us a bit about yourselves. Then we'll go around the room to introduce ourselves," said Ms. Battersby.

"I love music—especially percussion instruments like drums," signed Gabi. "I can feel the vibrations when they are played—especially when I'm standing on a wooden floor."

"And I love to sing," said Angie. "I sign while I sing so that people can hear and *see* my songs!"

The students all clapped to welcome their new classmates.

***

Later that day, the students were on the playground for recess. Gabi and Angie were playing on the swings.

Sadiq, Zaza, and Manny walked over to them after a game of basketball.

"Hi!" called Sadiq as they approached. "How's your first day going?"

Gabi signed, "We're both a little nervous. But we're happy to be here. This school seems really nice."

"So, you like to sing, Angie? That's neat," said Manny. "I can't sing at all!"

"And it's so cool that you love drums, Gabi. I do too!" said Sadiq. He made sure to face Gabi while he spoke so she could lip-read. "I want to learn how to play them."

Gabi's eyes lit up. "Yeah?" she signed. "I would love to be there for that!"

"There's a musical festival this weekend at my brother's school," said Sadiq. "Would you all like to come?"

"Yes!" said Zaza and Manny together. Then Zaza said, "Jinx!"

Angie and Gabi laughed. "Thanks for inviting us," said Angie. "It's very nice of you. We haven't made many friends yet."

Gabi smiled. "We'll be there," she signed. "As long as there will be drums!"

CHAPTER 3

HOOYO'S DURBAAN

"Ooh, what smells so good Hooyo?" asked Sadiq as he plopped down at the kitchen table.

"I am making *bariis* and *hilib*," replied Hooyo, smiling. "Your *baba's* favorite."

"It smells delicious," said Sadiq. He breathed deeply.

"How was your day, *qalbi*?" asked Hooyo. "Anything interesting happen?"

"Actually, yeah!" said Sadiq. "There are two new students in our class—Gabi and Angie. They're twins. They seem really nice."

"I hope you made them feel welcome, *wiilkeyga*?" said Hooyo.

Sadiq nodded. "Gabi is deaf and uses American Sign Language. She has a friend named Ms. Sarah who interprets for her. Angie loves to sing, and Gabi loves drums. She says she likes the feel of the vibrations they make. Isn't that cool? And also—"

"Slow down, qalbi!" said Hooyo, laughing. "You're talking a mile a minute! Why don't you take a breath."

"Sorry, Hooyo," said Sadiq, smiling. "I just got excited to tell you everything."

"That's okay," she said. "I know it's fun to make new friends."

"I invited them to the musical festival," said Sadiq. "Is that okay, Hooyo?"

"As long as their parents agree," she replied. "That was very nice of you."

"Isn't it neat that Gabi likes drums too?" said Sadiq, speaking quickly again.

"You know, qalbi," said Hooyo, "there are many percussion instruments in Somali music too."

"For real?" asked Sadiq.

"Yes—there is one called the *durbaan*. In fact, I have one in my closet. You can see it if you're careful with it. It's special because it was a gift from your *ayeeyo* on my wedding day."

"Can we go look at it now?" asked Sadiq. He could not wait to play a real Somali drum!

"Maybe after dinner, once you're done with dishes," Hooyo said with a wink.

"Deal," said Sadiq, grinning.

***

After dinner, Hooyo brought out the durbaan while the family gathered around her. It had a tall wooden base with leather stretched across the top.

"Now, remember what I told you," Hooyo said. "You have to be very careful with it. It's irreplaceable."

"Irreplaceable?" Sadiq asked.

"That means we can't get another one. It's one of a kind," explained Baba.

"We promise to be careful, Hooyo!" said Aliya.

"We can take turns. I bet Sadiq wants to go first," Nuurali said and smiled as he gently elbowed his brother.

"Can I?" asked Sadiq, jumping up. Rania and Amina bounced around him excitedly.

"Yes, but sit down," said Hooyo.

"And give him space, girls. Put the durbaan between your legs, Sadiq."

"Like this?" asked Sadiq. "I wish I was an octopus. I need more legs for this!"

Hooyo laughed. "Yes, just like that, qalbi."

Bam-ba-dum-da dum-dum boom! Sadiq gently patted out a rhythm on it.

"That was really good, Sadiq!" said Nuurali. "You're a natural!"

Sadiq beamed proudly. He played a bit more, getting the feel of the drum and trying various ways of hitting it to make different sounds.

"An excellent first effort, wiilkeyga. You've got good rhythm," said Baba, nodding.

"Now let your brother and sisters try," said Hooyo.

"Your turn, Aliya," said Sadiq.

"Like this?" Aliya asked.

"No, you have to put your leg here," explained Sadiq. "Like that."

"He thinks he's an expert already!" Nuurali teased.

The kids took turns playing the drum for the rest of the evening. Even Amina and Rania took turns, but then they got too silly. Hooyo said no more turns for them and put them to bed.

"Okay you three, it's your bedtime too," said Baba a while later.

"Please just five more minutes," pleaded Sadiq.

"You said that three times already, Sadiq," said Baba, laughing.

"Thank you, Hooyo," said Sadiq. "I love the durbaan. It's so cool."

"You're welcome, qalbi," she replied. "Make sure to put it in the back of the closet where it was. We don't want to trip over it."

"I will," said Sadiq.

In bed that night, Sadiq could not stop thinking about drumming. He liked the rhythms he could make with his hands and how happy it made him feel.

I have good rhythm, he thought, repeating Baba's compliment.

Tap-tap-ta-tap-ta ta ta-tap.

Sadiq lightly drummed on the wall next to him.

Rat-a-tat-ratta-tatta-tap-ta-tap.

"Will you please stop that?" Aliya groaned from the next room. "I can't sleep with all your drumming."

"A drummer's gotta drum!" said Sadiq.

"Go. To. Sleep," said Aliya.

"Good night," chuckled Sadiq. He turned over and went to sleep.

***

The next morning as Sadiq was getting dressed, he suddenly remembered something.

"It's my day for show and tell!" he said, bounding out of his room.

Aliya was standing in the hallway, waiting for her turn in the bathroom. "What are you going to bring?"

"I thought Hooyo's durbaan would be really cool to show," said Sadiq.

"You'll have to ask her first," Nuurali called out from the bathroom, sounding like his mouth was full of toothpaste.

"I'll go and ask her now!" said Sadiq.

"She already left for work," Aliya said. "She had an early meeting."

"What about Baba?" asked Sadiq.

"He's taking a shower downstairs," replied Nuurali as he came out of the bathroom. Aliya darted into it.

"You'll have to wait," Nuurali said as he went into his room and closed the door.

"I don't have time!" said Sadiq in a panic, but no one was listening. "Zaza and his mom will be here soon to take me to school."

HONK! HONK!

Oh no! They were already here! Sadiq didn't know what to do.

As long as I am careful, he thought, *it should be okay . . . . Hooyo won't even know it's gone.*

Sadiq went to his parents' bedroom and opened the closet door. He found the durbaan and carefully placed it in a large beach bag.

"Bye, Nuurali! Bye, Aliya!" Sadiq
called out. He ran out the door with
the beach bag.

CHAPTER 4

SHOW AND TELL TROUBLE

"So you have to sit on the floor like this," said Sadiq. "And then cross your legs halfway."

Sadiq was showing the class how to place the durbaan when playing.

"You put the drum between your legs," he continued. Then he demonstrated for the class.

Bam-ba-dum-da dum-dum boom!
Bam-ba-dum-da dum-dum boom!

"Well done, Sadiq!" said Ms. Battersby, clapping her hands. "How long have you been playing?"

"I only learned it yesterday," said Sadiq proudly. "I can teach you if you like."

"Maybe another time," said Ms. Battersby, smiling.

"It has such beautiful markings," signed Gabi.

"My hooyo says those are made by hand," said Sadiq.

"Wonderful show and tell," said Ms. Battersby. "You can go back to your desks. Let's all clap for Sadiq."

Soon it was time for lunch, and the students lined up outside the cafeteria.

"Look, Sadiq," said Zaza, pointing to a stack of flyers on a table. "Is that the festival you were talking about?"

Sadiq stopped to look. "Yes, that's the one!" he said excitedly and grabbed a flyer.

After they loaded up their trays with tacos, they found seats next to Gabi and Angie.

"Hi guys!" signed Gabi. The class had all learned how to sign hello, so the boys were eager to try out their new skill and sign back to her.

"What do you have, Sadiq?" Angie asked.

"It's the flyer for the festival," he said. "Would you like to see?"

"How cool!" Angie said. "There will be bands from ten different schools there!"

"Wow!" signed Gabi. "I can't wait to see the drum lines!"

"I like K-pop the best," said Angie. "I wonder if any of the bands will play that."

Zaza shrugged. "What about rock? I want to be a rock star when I grow up!"

"Since when?" asked Manny.

"Since I heard a new song in the car this morning!" Zaza said, and everyone laughed.

"I'm not sure if school bands play K-pop or rock," said Sadiq. "We'll have to go to the festival to find out!"

He picked up his lunch tray. "I need to head back to class to put away my drum.

See you guys later."

"See ya, Sadiq!" the kids called out and bit into their tacos.

***

Sadiq stared wide-eyed at the empty table. Ms. Battersby was not in the classroom. And neither was the durbaan.

"But . . . it was right there," he mumbled. "Where could it be?"

"I thought you were putting the drum away," said Manny as he walked into the classroom. Lunch period was over. Other students were coming back too.

"I was . . . I mean, I wanted to," stuttered Sadiq. "I left it right there on the table. But it's gone!"

"I am sure we can find it if we look," said Angie, peeking under a desk. "Did you ask Ms. Battersby?"

"I can't find her either," Sadiq said.

They spent several minutes looking for it, until someone walked into the classroom.

"Hello students, my name is Ms. Ricardo," she said as she set down a tall stack of books. "I am your substitute teacher. Ms. Battersby wasn't feeling well and went home to rest."

Sadiq slumped in his chair. "I am in so much trouble," he moaned to himself.

"It's reading time! Please come pick out a book from this stack," said Ms. Ricardo.

The other students all rushed over to the table, but Sadiq couldn't stop thinking about the durbaan.

"Don't worry, Sadiq," said Angie as she stopped by Sadiq's desk. "I am sure it will turn up. Maybe Ms. Battersby put it somewhere safe when she left."

"I didn't ask my mom for permission," admitted Sadiq, looking down at the desk. "I'll be in so much trouble."

***

That afternoon, Sadiq barely heard the lesson. Soon the bell rang, and it was time to go home.

"What will I tell Hooyo?" Sadiq asked Manny and Zaza.

"It will be okay," said Manny. "Just be honest."

Before he left, Sadiq checked the lost and found, but the durbaan wasn't there. He slowly walked out the door of the school. He didn't want to get to Hooyo's car.

Just then, Sadiq saw Ms. Ricardo walking out of school.

"Ms. Ricardo!" shouted Sadiq, waving his hand. "Can I ask you something?"

Sadiq jogged over to her. He talked to Ms. Ricardo for a moment, and then they walked back into the school together.

CHAPTER 5

LOST AND FOUND DRUM

"Hello, Hooyo!" shouted Sadiq. He ran as fast as he could to the car.

"Hello, Sadiq," said Hooyo. "Slow down, or you might trip and fall. And what are you carrying that's so big?"

Sadiq was panting as he got into the back seat.

"Is everything alright?" asked Hooyo.

"It is now," said Sadiq. He let out a huge sigh that he felt he had been holding in all afternoon. "I have bad news and good news."

"Okaaaaay . . ." said Hooyo. She turned off the car and turned to face him.

"The bad news is, I borrowed your durbaan without permission," said Sadiq, looking down. "I really wanted it for show and tell. But I couldn't ask you because you'd gone to work. So I took it. But then during lunch, the drum went missing."

"And what is the good news, please?" asked Hooyo. She had a worried look on her face.

"I found it!" exclaimed Sadiq. He opened the bag to show her. "Look Hooyo, nothing happened to it!"

"I see," said Hooyo, slowly.

"Ms. Ricardo, the sub, found it in the classroom after Ms. Battersby went home," Sadiq explained. "She thought it belonged in the music room and took it there. She didn't know it was mine."

"I am glad nothing happened," said Hooyo. "But I am very disappointed in you, Sadiq."

Sadiq nodded. "I know, Hooyo. I should have asked you first. I shouldn't have taken it."

"But . . . I am also very proud of you," said Hooyo.

"It must have been hard to own up," she continued. "And now you'll always remember how special this durbaan is."

"I will," said Sadiq, looking up.

"Come here, qalbi," said Hooyo. She held out her arms and gave Sadiq a big hug.

"I know you will take care of your instruments when you're older," said Hooyo. "And maybe you'll even have a drum of your own someday."

***

"Hi Zaza! Hi Manny!" Sadiq called out, waving to his friends as he and Nuurali arrived at the musical festival that weekend.

Nuurali dashed off when he saw his friend Malik. "Catch up with you later, Sadiq!" he said.

"Holy moly, this is amazing!" said Zaza as Sadiq approached. There were booths of different instruments to look at and try. Some were antique instruments. Some were unusual instruments. And some were really big. There was even a harp!

"Hey, that booth has guitar players!" said Zaza. "Let's go check that out later."

"I think I hear some drummers warming up," said Sadiq, looking around.

"There's Gabi and Angie!" said Manny. "Let's go hang out with them.

Why are they carrying balloons?"

"Hi guys!" said Angie.

"Have you been here long?" Gabi signed. "The schedule says the drum line starts soon! I am so excited!"

"We got here a little bit ago," said Sadiq. "What are the balloons for?"

"So I can feel the music with my hands! I brought extras so everyone can try it!" Gabi signed.

"That's so cool!" said Manny.

"Oh look, Sadiq!" said Angie. "That drum display over there has one that looks kind of like your mom's durbaan."

"You're right, it does!" said Sadiq, craning his neck to look.

Then he smiled with relief.

"But there's only one drum like my mom's," he said. "And thank goodness it's back at home, safe!"

Before he could explain how he'd found it, the drum line began marching past them. A shrill whistle blew, and then the drummers started clacking their drumsticks against the rims in a complicated rhythm. Then suddenly, the real drumming began.

Bada bada boom.

Bada bada boom.

Bada bada bada bada bada bada boom!

Sadiq looked over and saw a huge smile on Gabi's face. She handed out balloons to her friends.

Sadiq held the balloon and felt the vibrations on his hands. His jaw dropped at the feel of it.

"That's amazing!" he shouted over the drums.

Zaza and Manny started to dance with their balloons. Angie clapped along to the drumbeat, and Gabi held her balloon high over her head and bopped back and forth.

Sadiq couldn't stop smiling. *I can't wait to join band,* he thought.

GLOSSARY

American Sign Language (ASL)—a way of communicating using gestures, movements, and expressions

antique (ann-TEEK)—from an earlier time

brass (BRASS)—a group of musical wind instruments made of metal

clarinet (klair-uh-NET)—a tube-shaped wind instrument made of wood or plastic with keys and holes that create notes when pushed

instrument (IN-struh-ment)—a device used to produce music

interpret (in-TERR-pret)—to explain or tell the meaning

irreplaceable (ih-rih-PLAY-sub-buhl)—not able to be replaced

lip-read (LIP-reed)—to understand speech by watching someone's lips move as they talk

nervous (NER-vuss)—feeling uneasy or scared

panic (PAN-ik)—a sudden worry or fright

percussion (per-KUH-shun)—a type of musical instrument that you beat or strike to play

permission (per-MIH-shun)—consent or approval to do something

reed (REED)—a thin piece of wood that goes on the mouthpiece of some instruments to help make sound

substitute (SUB-stih-toot)—a short-term replacement

vibration (vye-BRAY-shun)—quivering, trembling, or shaking that can be felt

woodwind (WOOD-wind)—a group of musical wind instruments that use keys and holes to produce different sounds

TALK ABOUT IT

1. Sadiq takes Hooyo's durbaan without asking her. Have you ever taken something from your parents or siblings without permission? What happened? How did they feel about it when they found out?

2. Is there any special musical instrument in your family's culture? What is it called and what type of instrument is it? (Wind, brass, or percussion?)

3. Gabi and Angie are new students in Sadiq's class. Think of a time when you made friends with new students or new neighbors. Was it easy or hard? Did you find that you had something in common?

WRITE IT DOWN

1. Do you have a favorite band? Write a letter to them asking what it's like being in a band. Is it a lot of work? What is it like traveling to concerts and festivals and performing?

2. Musical instruments are often used to accompany a song. Come up with a song of your own and write down the lyrics.

3. If you were starting a band, what would you need to do? Write down how many members you would need in your band. What instrument would each person play? Would you also have a singer? What kind of music would your band play?

MAKE SOME DRUMS!

Sadiq can't wait to join a band. How about you? With the help of an adult, make your own drum set and imagine you are playing on stage in front of a cheering crowd!

Try these different drum designs. For each one, use pencils, pens, chopsticks, or just your hands as drumsticks!

BUCKET DRUMS

WHAT YOU NEED:

- one or more large buckets

WHAT YOU DO:

1. Flip the buckets upside down.

2. Use your hands or makeshift drumsticks to try to play your favorite song!

CYLINDER DRUMS

WHAT YOU NEED:

- empty aluminum cans or oatmeal containers
- balloons
- rubber bands

WHAT YOU DO:

1. Ask an adult to wash out the cans or containers.

2. Cut the bottom tip off a balloon. Pull the rest of the balloon over the top of one container.

3. Secure a rubber band around the balloon to keep it from slipping off the container. Repeat for each can or container.

4. Practice your rhythm!

BONGO BOWLS

WHAT YOU NEED:

- paper bowls
- tape

WHAT YOU DO:

1. Tape the tops of two paper bowls together, face to face.

2. Repeat step one so you have two drums.

3. Invite your friends to join your band!

CREATORS

Siman Nuurali grew up in Kenya. She now lives in Minnesota. Siman and her family are Somali—just like Sadiq and his family! She and her five children love to play badminton and board games together. Siman works at Children's Hospital and, in her free time, she enjoys writing and reading.

Christos Skaltsas was born and raised in Athens, Greece. For the past fifteen years, he has worked as a freelance illustrator for children's book publishers. In his free time, he loves playing with his son, collecting vinyl records, and traveling around the world.